SWIMMING
THE DISTANCE

BY JAKE MADDOX

text by
Michael Anthony Steele

STONE ARCH BOOKS
a capstone imprint

Jake Maddox JV books are published by Stone Arch Books
A Capstone Imprint
1710 Roe Crest Drive
North Mankato, Minnesota 56003
www.capstonepub.com

Library of Congress Cataloging-in-Publication Data

Maddox, Jake, author.
 Swimming the distance / by Jake Maddox ; text by Michael Anthony Steele.
   pages cm. -- (Jake Maddox JV)
 Summary: Mason Williams is on his junior high school swim team, and he has always
been fast at the short distances, but if he wants to compete in the longer races he will need to
work on his endurance — so his best friend suggests that he train in the nearby lake.
 ISBN 978-1-4342-9637-5 (library binding) -- ISBN 978-1-4342-9669-6 (pbk.) -- ISBN 978-1-
4965-0178-3 (ebook PDF)
1. Swimming--Juvenile fiction. 2. Swimming--Training--Juvenile fiction. 3. Competition
(Psychology)--Juvenile fiction. 4. Physical fitness--Juvenile fiction. 5. Best friends--Juvenile
fiction. [1. Swimming--Fiction. 2. Competition (Psychology)--Fiction. 3. Physical fitness--
Fiction. 4. Best friends--Fiction. 5. Friendship--Fiction.] I. Steele, Michael Anthony, author.
II. Title.

PZ7.M25643Sw 2015
813.6--dc23

                                    2014023846

This book has been officially leveled by using the F&P Text Level Gradient™
Leveling System.

Art Director: Heather Kindseth
Designer: Veronica Scott
Production Specialist: Jennifer Walker

Photo Credits:
Shutterstock: Bedrin, chapter openings, S.Pytel, cover, Tom Wang, back cover
Design Elements: Shutterstock

Printed in the United States of America.
042017   010462R

TABLE OF CONTENTS

CHAPTER 1

OUT OF BREATH

BEEEEEEEEP!

The buzzer sounded, and Mason Williams launched off the blocks to start his fifty-meter freestyle race. Every muscle in his body tensed as Mason dove into the cool water. Once submerged, he leveled out just under the surface. Staying underwater at the beginning of a race gave swimmers an edge. Mason grabbed three perfect strokes before coming up for air.

Once he was back at the surface, Mason focused on performing each freestyle stroke perfectly. He kicked his legs for added speed, but they mainly kept his body straight while his arms did most of the work to move him forward.

Even though it was Mason's first year on the junior high swim team, he wasn't new to swimming. He had taken swimming lessons for years at summer camp, and he frequently visited the local lake with his best friend Alex during the warm months when school was still in session.

Mason knew he had some work to do on his technique, but with each race, he found it easier and easier to maintain his form. *I need to make the most of every stroke,* he thought as he cut through the water.

Once a stroke was complete, Mason made sure to keep his arm close to his body as he brought it around and then eventually up for another stroke. Every movement had to be focused on pushing his body quickly through the water without causing any drag between strokes.

Just one flip turn, and then I'm in the home stretch, Mason thought as he approached the pool's edge. The key to perfecting a flip turn was to keep up as much speed as possible approaching the wall of the pool, and after the push-off, to straighten the body and pull the arms in to prevent drag.

At the last second, Mason brought his arms to his sides and performed an underwater somersault. Once his body was facing the opposite direction, he brought his legs up and pushed off from the cement wall of the pool with both feet. The technique, if done correctly, allowed a swimmer to switch directions as smoothly as possible.

Mason didn't have to think much as he sped underwater, spiraling until he was right side up again. He was a natural at flip turns. However, once he broke the surface and took a quick breath, he returned to concentrating on his form.

Stroke, stroke, breathe. Stroke, stroke, breathe.

Mason poured on the speed. He didn't think about the swimmers on either side of him. Instead he focused on his technique and the goal before him — to dominate another race.

Just two more strokes and Mason's outstretched hand caught the edge of the pool. He popped his head out of the water to find himself alone at the finish line. A half-second later, the rest of the swimmers touched the wall. They were too late, though. Mason had won.

Out of breath, Mason pulled himself onto the edge of the pool. As he removed his goggles and swim cap, he felt a sharp slap on his back.

"Great job, Mason," said Coach Wilson. He threw a towel over Mason's shoulder. "Another first-place finish."

Mason got to his feet. "Thanks, Coach," he said between breaths. He toweled off his torso first, hoping to hide the fact that his chest was heaving as he caught his breath.

"Take a break," Coach Wilson said. "You've earned it."

Mason nodded and followed Coach Wilson over to where the rest of Gilmer Junior High School's swim team was stationed. They took up a small corner of the school's natatorium. The large building echoed with chatter and cheering from the stands and hollering from the teams and coaches. It seemed that the only quiet place in the entire building was underwater.

Mason weaved through the oncoming swimmers who were making their way to the starting blocks for the next race, the one-hundred-meter freestyle. He stopped when Josh, his team's captain, stepped in front of him with at an outstretched fist. Mason shifted the towel to his left hand and returned the fist bump with his right hand.

"Good job, dude," Josh said. The taller boy was already wearing his swim cap and goggles.

Mason's chest rose and fell as he tried to catch his breath. "Thanks," he managed to say.

Josh stood there, watching Mason grab a couple more quick breaths. "You're going to have to work on your endurance if you're ever going to swim with us big fish," Josh said.

Mason willed himself to inhale as quietly as possible. But it wasn't easy to breathe normally when you had to think about it.

Josh smirked and continued walking toward the starting blocks at the edge of the pool. After the older boy had passed, Mason put on his robe and sat down to watch the next race with the rest of his team. Josh was the team's best swimmer, especially at the one-hundred-meter distance. As usual, he would probably smoke the competition in this race.

Mason took some comfort in the fact that he could match the team captain when it came to short races like the fifty-meter freestyle he'd just won. Just two laps of the twenty-five meter-long pool — it should be no sweat.

But Mason knew that his stamina was weak, especially when it came to longer distances such as the one-hundred or two-hundred-meter freestyle. In fact, by the time Josh was in the lead on the fourth lap of the one-hundred-meter race, Mason was just beginning to breathe normally as he recovered from his fifty-meter distance.

Mason applauded and cheered with the rest of his team as Josh finished first in the one-hundred-meter freestyle. Then he took a long, slow breath. *Josh is right,* he thought. *If I ever want to swim with the big fish, I'm going to have to work on my endurance.*

CHAPTER 2

WATER IS WATER

The next day, Mason was tired. He decided to take the day off, even though he usually went to the junior high's pool every Sunday, when it was open to the public, to get in some extra practice.

Instead, Mason spent the afternoon at his best friend Alex's house, helping him practice for his part in the upcoming school play.

"The dragon sword!" shouted Alex. "Forged in Atlantis! Bewitched by the dark wizard, Shantor! And honed to a fine edge by a red dragon's fiery breath!"

Alex paused and gazed up at the small wooden ruler — his sword — he had clasped in both hands. "Line?" he asked, shooting a glance at Mason.

Alex had been involved in Gilmer Junior High's drama department ever since he and Mason had started going to school there. And he'd been involved in community theater even before that. As his best friend since elementary school, Mason had always helped him rehearse.

This play was one of the most important shows Alex had ever been a part of. As the school year wound down, the drama department was preparing for its biggest production yet. The play was going to be full of knights, swordplay, and even a cool special-effects dragon.

Alex had been practicing for months, but with opening night less than two weeks away, he seemed more nervous as each day crept forward.

Mason sighed and read the next line for his friend. "The sword of my father."

Alex raised the ruler higher. "The sword," he boomed, "of my father!"

"Why do you always forget that part?" asked Mason. "It seems pretty important."

"I know, right? It's a major plot point and everything." Alex tossed the ruler onto his desk and plopped down onto his bed. "I think I'm too worried about remembering the name Shantor. What kind of name is that anyway?"

Mason shrugged. "It's a good dark wizard name," he replied.

"Yeah, I guess Steve wouldn't have the same punch," said Alex.

Mason laughed and closed the book he'd been following along from. "You only forgot a couple of lines this time," he said. "I think you're ready."

"Man, I don't feel ready," admitted Alex. "Even though I'm just the understudy, I have to be 100 percent ready in case Jeremy catches a cold or something."

"What's the chance that will happen?" asked Mason.

Alex shrugged. "Well, since I can't get him to lick a single dirty doorknob . . ."

Mason laughed. "You want the part that badly?" he asked.

"I don't want him to get sick on purpose," explained Alex. "But it would be sweet to be the star of the show for a change, instead of someone in the background or behind the scenes."

Mason shook his head. "I don't know how you can do that," he said. "Stand on a stage with all those people watching you."

"Aren't there tons of people watching you during your swim meets?" asked Alex.

Mason nodded. "Yeah," he replied, "but that's different. I'm too focused on the race to even notice them."

"It's the same for me," said Alex. "Except I focus on the character I'm playing."

Mason shook his head and said, "I guess I'd have to be a drama geek to understand." He shot Alex a good-natured smile.

Alex laughed. "Yeah, you dumb jocks just don't get it," he said.

Mason laughed at the friendly dig, but it was true — he really didn't get it. Even though he and Alex had been best friends since elementary school, they were worlds apart. Alex enjoyed being the center of attention. He always had a joke or a snappy comeback ready. Sometimes those jokes got the two of them in trouble in class — Alex for making the jokes and Mason for laughing too hard at them.

Mason, on the other hand, had always been more quiet and reserved. He enjoyed sports because he was part of a team — not the center of attention. Even in the pool, he was always surrounded by teammates and opponents in other lanes. Mason also liked sports because they encouraged him to push himself, to make sure every movement was precise and calculated. That quality had helped him excel in soccer, basketball, and even track and field. But swimming had turned out to be the perfect sport for him — it was a competition where every movement had to be almost perfect.

Alex, who had never been one for sports, always said that there was no sense in moving fast unless someone was chasing you.

"Are you ready to work on the next scene?" asked Alex.

"Sure," replied Mason. "What are friends for?"

"Too bad I can't help you train for your swim meets," Alex replied.

"I know," said Mason. "But the whole town seems to use the school's natatorium. Between all the swimming lessons and water aerobics classes that go on, there's only an hour of free swim each night."

"And I bet it's hard to swim laps when you're dodging kids with water wings and scuba flippers," Alex added.

"You got that right," Mason agreed.

Alex stood and gazed out his bedroom window. "So you need a place to swim undisturbed, right?" he asked.

"Yeah . . ." Mason said hesitantly.

Alex raised his eyebrows and gestured to something outside the window.

Mason stood. "What? You get a pool put in and didn't tell me?" he joked.

Alex rolled his eyes. "No, dude. The lake."

Mason joined him at the window. Alex's family lived close to Black Bear Lake. He could just see the water from Alex's bedroom window. The two of them had spent many summer days swimming, camping, and boating in and around the lake. At first, they'd go with their families, and then when they were old enough, they went by themselves.

"Really?" Mason asked. "You think I should train in the lake?"

"Water is water, right?" asked Alex.

"I'm not sure it's so safe," said Mason. "For swim training, anyway."

"Sure it is," said Alex. "We can use the buddy system."

Mason and Alex had learned about the buddy system during their first year at summer camp. Whether they swam in the pool or the lake, they always had to have a buddy no matter what. If you got out to use the bathroom, your buddy had to get out, too. The lifeguards even routinely blew their whistles for a "buddy check." That meant that all the swimmers had to grab their buddy's hand and raise it up high. By the end of the first free swim, all the campers knew the buddy system.

Alex hadn't been the best swimmer at first, so the buddy system had been especially helpful to him.

Mason had taken to it quickly and helped boost Alex's confidence by teaching him different strokes. Now, however, both of the boys were excellent swimmers, and their parents trusted them to stay safe in and around the water.

"Okay, the buddy system. Right," said Mason. "So does that mean you're going to train with me?"

Alex looked surprised. "Train with you?" he asked. "I'm only swimming fast if I'm being chased by sharks."

"Then how can we practice the buddy system?" asked Mason.

"I have something else in mind," Alex said with a smile. "It'll be just you, me, and the Green Avenger."

Mason laughed. The Green Avenger was what Alex had named his green kayak. It might not be the usual buddy system, but Mason thought Alex's plan just might work.

CHAPTER 3

THE BUDDY SYSTEM

The next afternoon, Mason cut through the dark lake water. The surface of the lake wasn't as calm as the pool, but it didn't bother him. After all, a pool could get rough during a race sometimes. All of those racers zipping through their lanes didn't make for very calm water.

The choppy lake water will be perfect for my stamina training, Mason thought. *After all, don't professional track runners practice running with leg weights so they feel lighter when they race? This is kind of like that.*

Mason had been swimming nonstop for a half hour. He felt a little short of breath and decided to take a break. He stopped and treaded water for a moment as Alex's long green kayak pulled up alongside him. Mason grabbed the hull of the Green Avenger and pulled up his goggles.

"Well?" asked Alex. "What do you think?"

Mason caught his breath before answering. "Not bad," he replied. "Pretty cool, actually."

Alex lowered his paddle and gave a small bow. "You're welcome," he said. His bulky life vest rode up to cover his chin as he bent low.

The boys always wore their vests when they kayaked. In fact, Mason's life vest, along with a round lifesaver and a rope, was tucked away in the kayak just in case they ran into trouble while he was swimming.

Training in the lake is a great idea after all, Mason thought as he rested. *Alex and I know the area like the backs of our hands.*

Since Alex had gotten his kayak last summer, he and Mason had paddled all over the lake. It was a two-person open-cockpit kayak. Instead of having a port for each paddler's seat, it had a large opening across the kayak's deck. The boat looked like a long, flat canoe. The extra space was great for carrying their packs when they went camping on one of the lake's little islands.

Alex glanced at the open water. "How far do you want to go?" he asked.

Mason looked out past the kayak. Black Bear was a large lake. Since it was a weekday, there weren't any water-skiers or speedboats out, and the few boats that were out on the water were mostly hugging the shores. Mason and Alex had almost the entire lake to themselves.

"How about we follow the shore down to the old dam and back?" asked Mason. "That should give us plenty of practice time before it gets dark."

"Sounds good," said Alex.

"Do you think we could do this the rest of the week?" asked Mason. "We could start earlier tomorrow after school."

"As long as you save some time to help me run lines for the play," said Alex.

"You bet," agreed Mason. He pushed off the kayak and treaded water once more.

"In the meantime," said Alex, clearing his throat dramatically, "I can work on the songs." Alex inhaled deeply and began to sing.

Mason rolled his eyes and laughed. He'd forgotten that Alex's play was a musical. "Drama geek," he teased, adjusting his goggles.

Alex shook his head and began paddling. "Just keep swimming, ya dumb jock."

Mason rolled over and continued to swim toward the middle of the lake. He tuned out Alex's singing and concentrated on his strokes. This kind of training wasn't about speed. It was about building up his endurance. Mason would swim as long as possible and make sure every stroke, kick, and breath was performed perfectly. If he kept at it, he would build up his strength in no time.

Stroke, stroke, breathe. Stroke, stroke, breathe.

Mason kicked his feet rhythmically. He wanted to push himself to be more than just a sprinter who could swim fifty-meter races. If he worked hard enough, he knew he had a chance for a spot in a one-hundred-meter race. *How cool would that be?* Mason thought.

Stroke, stroke, breathe. Stroke, stroke, breathe.

And if I work even harder, thought Mason, *maybe, just maybe, I could swim a two-hundred-meter race by the end of the season. What would Josh think of that?*

Stroke, stroke, breathe. Stroke, stroke, breathe.

I know it won't be easy, but if I keep up this training, Mason thought, *I'll be swimming with the big fish in no time.*

CHAPTER 4

PROGRESS

For the rest of the school week, Mason and Alex kept up the training. After school and regular swim practice, Mason would bike over to Alex's house, and the two of them would hit the lake.

On Tuesday, their second time out, Mason had swum all the way to the old dam and back. Over the next couple of days, he found that he didn't have to take as many breaks. It was working. Mason's stamina was increasing.

During swim team practices that week, Mason tried to work on his speed. Each practice, Coach Wilson had the team swim laps and timed each swimmer to check his progress. Mason was getting faster, and he was also no longer wiped out after just a couple of laps.

On Friday, Coach had a time trial for the one-hundred-meter freestyle. Mason finished just behind Josh, the best swimmer on their team at that distance. At the end of practice that day, Coach Wilson called Mason over.

"That time trial was impressive, Mason," he said. "And your laps have been getting faster every day this week."

"Thanks, Coach," Mason said. "I've been practicing really hard, and I feel much stronger."

Coach frowned, deep in thought, as he looked over some notes on his clipboard. "Well," he said, "let's try you out in the one-hundred-meter freestyle tomorrow." He looked up and smiled.

Mason grinned back at him. He just hoped he was ready — tomorrow was going to be big.

* * *

The next day, Mason's heart pounded as he completed a flip turn, pushed off the wall, and began the final lap of the one-hundred-meter race.

His legs felt like noodles, and his shoulder muscles burned, but he tried not to pay attention to any of those things. He poured on the speed toward the finish line. This was his first one-hundred-meter race, and it was time to see if all his training that week would pay off.

Mason rolled his body with each stroke, keeping his hands cupped and kicking his legs with enough force to keep his body in position. He had to split his concentration between maintaining his form and increasing his speed, which was difficult since he was almost out of energy. It was harder to breathe. Mason felt as if he wasn't getting enough air during the brief moment when he turned his face out of the water. Still, he forced those thoughts out of his mind as he sliced through the water toward the edge of the pool.

Suddenly, Mason's hand hit the side, and he popped his head out of the water. He glanced to his right and left and saw that he wasn't alone. Two swimmers bobbed, one on either side of him.

Were they already here? Did I come in third? Mason wondered as he tried to control his heavy breathing. Usually he could tell how well he did when he finished, but today he had no clue. It must've been a close race.

A split second later, the rest of the swimmers finished. Everyone looked up at the scoreboard to see who won. It seemed like hours passed before their names popped up. Finally, the scoreboard lit up, and Mason's name appeared at the top. His team cheered. Mason had won the race!

Mason climbed out of the pool and went to his team's corner. He was drained, but he managed to return the high fives from his teammates.

"Great job, Mason," said Coach Wilson. "It was a close one, but you did it."

"Thanks," Mason managed to say.

Coach clapped his hands and said, "All right! Josh, Brian. You two are up for the two hundred."

Josh and Brian pulled off their sweats, put on their swim caps, and headed for the pool.

Josh brushed by Mason. "I didn't think you had it in you," he said with a smirk. "But not quite a big fish yet. You'll have to be better if you want to swim the two hundred."

"Speaking of," Brian chimed in, "you might get a chance soon. I might not make the meet next weekend, and Coach will need another swimmer."

Mason nodded but didn't reply. He still hadn't caught his breath. Instead, he glanced up at the stands, thinking about his next goal. He spotted his mom and dad, with Alex sitting beside them. Mason's parents each gave him a thumbs-up. Alex nodded his head and gave a knowing smile.

Mason smiled back. *Two hundred, here I come,* he thought.

CHAPTER 5

SWAMPED

On Tuesday afternoon, just a few days after his big win in the one-hundred-meter freestyle, Mason hung off the side of Alex's kayak as it bobbed up and down in the rough lake water.

"Looking good, man," said Alex. He rested his paddle on his lap. "You're barely breathing hard."

"I'm getting there," said Mason.

Mason and Alex had spent every afternoon on the lake since the meet on Saturday, and Mason could feel himself getting stronger.

Alex glanced around. "Do you think we should call it quits for the day?" he asked. "The wind's picking up. It's getting harder to paddle in a straight line."

Mason knew why. The kayak's open cockpit was great for gear, but unfortunately, it was also great for catching wind. During a really windy day last summer, Alex and Mason had struggled to steer it, and they'd almost capsized.

"Just a little more, okay?" asked Mason.

Alex rolled his eyes. "All right. But you owe me. We haven't run lines in a week. I have the script in my dry bag if you wanna take a quick break."

Mason pulled down his goggles and pushed away from the kayak. "You memorized everything already," he said. "You got this."

"Yeah, but I don't feel like I do," Alex said. "What if I freeze up?"

Mason began a backstroke. "You won't."

Before Alex could argue, Mason rolled over again and began his front crawl. He planned to pick up the speed a little. However, after a couple of strokes, he realized that Alex was right. The wind had picked up, and Mason found himself battling small whitecaps as the blustery weather churned up the lake's surface. He had to time his breaths carefully so he didn't breathe in water.

Even so, he kept going. Mason enjoyed the challenge. It helped him focus. He liked to push himself. He knew it was the best way to improve.

After a few more strokes, Mason glanced over his shoulder at Alex. Instead of being directly behind him as usual, his friend was several feet back and facing the wrong direction. Alex grimaced as he dug his paddle deep into the water. He tried to turn toward Mason but couldn't. Alex looked up at Mason. "A little help, maybe?"

Mason spun around and swam back toward the kayak. He'd almost reached his friend when a gust of wind came out of nowhere and knocked Alex off balance. The kayak capsized, and Mason's best friend fell into the churning lake.

CHAPTER 6

OVERBOARD

"Alex!" shouted Mason. He kicked hard, darting through the choppy water.

Alex popped to the surface a few feet away from the kayak. His life vest had done its job. With his paddle in hand, he swam toward the overturned kayak. "I'm okay," he said.

After he saw that Alex was all right, Mason changed course and swam for a red object floating in the lake — it was Alex's dry bag, a special plastic bag that kept their phones and other personal items dry.

Mason made his way through the rough water and grabbed the bag. He wrapped his arms around it and used it as a float. Then he kicked his way back to Alex and the kayak.

Both boys reached the upturned kayak and latched on, bobbing along in the rough water.

Alex shook his head and said, "I'm not going to say I told you so . . ."

Mason sighed. "Yeah, you are."

Alex smiled. "You're right, I am. I told you so." He looked up at the sky and shook his head again. "I told you, told you, told you so."

"All right, all right," said Mason. "Enough with the drama, drama geek. The dumb jock was dumb. My bad."

Alex raised an eyebrow. "I can live with that." He smiled and shot a thumb over his shoulder. "Let's get to shore."

Holding onto either side of the kayak, they slowly swam toward the bank. When they were in shallow water, they stood and carried the long boat to the shore. Dumping water out of the kayak was nothing new. They had capsized the boat while goofing around at the lake before.

Once all the water was out, Alex climbed back into the kayak. "Should we call it a day?" he asked. "This wind is crazy."

"I have an idea," said Mason. "I'm coming in." Alex leaned the kayak to one side so Mason could climb into the other seat. "How about the island? It's usually not as windy over there."

"You're kidding, right?" asked Alex. He held up both arms. "I'm soaked here."

Mason smiled. "Hey, me too," he said. "But you don't hear me complaining."

"Ha, ha," said Alex.

"Come on, I really need the practice," Mason said. "Brian told me he might not make it to the meet this Saturday. And if that's true, then there will be a spot open for the two-hundred-meter freestyle. This could be my chance. I have to be ready."

Alex stared at Mason for a moment. Then he rolled his eyes and reached down the side of the kayak. He picked up the spare paddle and held it out. "All right," he said.

"Thanks, man," said Mason. He pulled on the spare life vest and together they paddled along the shore.

Near the north end of Black Bear Lake, the large body of water narrowed. The banks rose up higher, and a thick forest lined each shore. More than likely, these obstacles would help block the wind.

The water should be calmer there, Mason thought. Besides, he and Alex knew that area well. Their main camping island jutted out into that narrow part of the lake.

Soon the small landmass came into view. Even though there wasn't much to it, the island was covered with the same tall trees that lined the lakeshores.

Mason's shoulder muscles burned from paddling. "Man, I forgot that this is a workout, too," he said.

"Thank you," said Alex. "I'm glad you see that it's not all fun and games following you all over the lake."

"Yeah, yeah," said Mason. "Want to take a break on the island?"

"Definitely," replied Alex.

They beached the kayak, hopped out, and pulled it ashore. Then they both plopped down on a large log that sat a several feet back from the water.

While Alex dug through his dry bag, Mason stared out at the lake. *The water's smoother in the inlet, that's for sure,* he thought as he looked toward the mainland shore opposite them. He recognized the mountain bike trail on the other side. He and Alex often spent the warm months riding their mountain bikes up and down those wooded trails. The shore across the lake was a good distance away.

Maybe the perfect distance, Mason thought.

"How far do you think the other shore is?" asked Mason, emerging from his thoughts.

Alex glanced up and shrugged his shoulders. "I don't know."

"Would you say it's about the length of two football fields?" asked Mason.

Alex squinted his eyes as he stared out toward the opposite shore. "Two football fields? Yeah, I guess so. Maybe a little more. Why?"

Mason stood up. "Then swimming there and back would be a little over four hundred meters, right?" he asked. "That would be good training — double the length of a two-hundred-meter race."

One race on the way out, one on the way back, Mason thought.

"Not so fast there," said Alex. "At least let my shorts dry out first."

Mason shook his head and returned to his seat on the log. "All right."

"In the meantime . . ." Alex said, pulling out a stack of papers from his dry bag. "Let's run some lines."

CHAPTER 7

ABOUT TIME

During Thursday afternoon's practice, Mason swam laps with the rest of the team. As he neared the edge of the pool, he heard the muffled sound of Coach Wilson's whistle. Mason stopped swimming and popped his head out of the water.

"Okay, that's enough laps for now," Coach hollered. "Everyone huddle up."

Mason and his teammates climbed out of the pool. They all grabbed their towels and gathered around the coach.

"The roster is pretty much set for Saturday's swim meet," Coach Wilson said, "but Brian's going out of town on a family trip, so I want to rotate one of you into the two-hundred-meter freestyle with Josh. We'll do a time trial to see who gets the spot." He looked around at the boys' faces. "Who's up for the challenge?"

Mark and Eddie put their hands up right away.

"All right, Mark," said the coach. "Since Eddie just finished some sprints, I'll have you swim the time trial first while he rests."

Coach grabbed the stopwatch hanging from his neck. "I'll run you one at a time so I can check your exact splits," he said.

As Mark got ready, the rest of the team moved to the nearby bleachers. Mason hung back. "I'd like to try, Coach," he said.

Coach raised an eyebrow. "For a minute there, I didn't think you were going to say anything."

"I think I'm ready," said Mason.

Coach patted him on the shoulder. "Okay, then," he said. "You're up after Eddie."

Mason wrapped his towel around his shoulders and joined the rest of the team. As he took a seat, he caught Josh's eye.

"So, you're going for it, huh?" asked Josh.

Mason nodded. "That's right."

Josh shrugged. "We'll see how big a fish you are," he said.

Mason tried to put Josh out of his mind. For a team captain, he wasn't very supportive of some of the swimmers. Instead, Mason turned his attention to Mark, the first of the three volunteers.

Unfortunately for Mark, he wasn't a great starter. The key to a good start was getting into a crouching position and leaning off the starting block as far as possible without falling in. Then the swimmer's body should be like a coiled spring ready to pop at the sound of the starting buzzer. But Mark's posture was slouched as he climbed onto the starting block and bent halfheartedly into starting position.

"On your mark," said the coach. "Get set . . ."

He put his whistle to his lips.

BLEEEEEEEEET!

Mark hesitated before diving into the pool. Mason knew that would cost him some time. In the end, it did.

After Mark completed all eight laps, the coach looked at his stopwatch. "Two minutes, twenty-eight seconds," he said.

Mark looked a little disappointed with his time, and he climbed out of the pool slowly.

Next up was Eddie. Eddie was like Mason — a great sprinter. He was best in relay races, which included several swimmers swimming different laps of the same race.

Maybe that's why Eddie isn't great at flip turns, Mason thought. *He only has to do one turn in a relay.* In a relay race, the starting swimmer would cover the length of the pool, turn, and then swim back to a teammate who would continue the race. Sometimes the swimmers all swam the same stroke, and sometimes they swam different ones.

Coach blew his whistle, and Eddie dove into the pool. He had a great start and cut through the water with ease. When he reached the other side of the pool, he dove underwater.

Looks like he started that turn a little too soon, Mason thought. When Eddie pushed off from the other side of the pool, he barely seemed to move. Since he was too far away from the edge when he turned, his legs didn't push him very far.

The rest of Eddie's time trial went the same way. He didn't quite have the flip turns down. On his final lap, he tried to make up for it. But during the last turn, he waited too long to flip. His feet became jumbled, and he had to kick twice to push away from the edge. All of those bad turns had cost him precious seconds. Mason could tell by the coach's face that they had cost too much.

"Two minutes, twenty seconds," Coach said.

Finally, it was Mason's turn. He just hoped that all of his practice at the lake made up for his personal weakness — stamina.

Mason stepped up on the starting block and got into position. Luckily for Mason, he'd never had a problem starting a race. Coach Wilson had drilled them at the beginning of the season, and Mason had practiced diving into the pool nonstop. It hadn't taken him long to lock down the technique.

Mason leaned over the water as far as he could. He wanted to give himself every advantage on his start.

BLEEEEEEEEET!

Mason launched into the air before the whistle had stopped. He dove under the surface and was already up swimming before the sound echoed away in the large natatorium. Mason knew this race wasn't a sprint, which meant that he needed to pace himself. He couldn't put everything he had into the first few laps. If he did, he would tire out too early. Instead, he concentrated on his technique.

Mason made sure each hand cupped the maximum amount of water as he swam along. He spun his body just enough to let his arm come out of the water and reach forward for another stroke so it didn't hit the water and add drag. He made sure to inhale and exhale at just the right moments between strokes. His legs kicked rhythmically, moving his body forward and keeping his position in the water.

When Mason came to the first turn, he dove underwater, keeping just enough space between himself and the wall so he could flip his body around.

Now it was time to really put his legs to work. Both feet found the wall of the pool, and Mason pushed off hard. He rocketed through the water, spinning back into position. His lead arm shot out of the water, and he continued his precise strokes.

As Mason swam the first five laps, he carefully increased his speed. By the middle of the sixth lap, he could feel his heart hammering in his chest. Normally by this time, he would have been almost spent. But thanks to his training, Mason felt a well of energy buried deep inside him. He tapped that well and pushed off the wall into the seventh lap.

Mason dialed up the speed some more. He knew he had to swim the entire length of the pool and back once more before it was over. He hoped he had enough energy left.

After the final turn, Mason went for it. He swam as fast as he could toward the finish. He concentrated on speed, but his form began to slip. His arm dipped too low as he reached forward, dragging through the water. He could feel himself slowing down.

Mason forced himself to focus on the strokes once more. Unfortunately, the more he focused on technique, the less he thought about speed. Now he wasn't swimming as fast as he could. Mason tried to speed up again. This time, his ankles bumped together. He desperately tried to balance form and speed as he swam the final fifty meters.

"Time!" yelled Coach Wilson as Mason's hand hit the edge of the pool.

Gasping for breath, Mason clung to the side and slowly removed his goggles.

"Well, well, well," said the coach. "Two minutes, fourteen seconds. Looks like we have ourselves a new distance swimmer."

Mason took some deep breaths and smiled as his team applauded.

"Look out, Josh," said Coach Wilson. "He's creeping up on your time."

"Finally," replied Josh with a smirk. "About time we had some competition around here."

Mason couldn't reply; he was too out of breath. *You're going to have some competition, all right,* he thought.

CHAPTER 8

BUDDY CHECK

After practice, Mason made his way to the drama department to catch up with Alex. As he shuffled down the empty hallway, his leg muscles burned, and his arms felt like spaghetti. Nevertheless, he was in a great mood. He had finally built up enough stamina to swim in a two-hundred-meter race. He'd even come close to matching Josh's time. *All that work in the lake finally paid off,* Mason thought.

But Mason had a feeling that just a little more training would take him over the top. He felt as if he had a real chance at winning the two-hundred-meter race in the upcoming meet on Saturday.

If Alex and I go out today, I could get one more session in, Mason thought. *Then on Friday, I could take the day off and let my body recover. Everything could work out perfectly.*

Mason spotted Alex exiting the theater. "Guess who's racing the two-hundred-meter freestyle on Saturday?" Mason asked.

Alex turned around slowly, his face pale. "Jeremy has the flu," he said.

Mason's eyes widened. "Dude, you look like *you* have the flu."

"Jeremy has the flu," repeated Alex. "The lead in the play has the flu."

Mason finally realized what Alex was trying to say. He grinned and said, "That's great, dude." Then he cringed. "Well, not so great for Jeremy. But that means you're going on, right? You're going to be the star of the show!"

"You bet that's what it means," said Alex.

"Congratulations," said Mason. He clapped a hand on his friend's shoulder. "And even though I know most of the lines by heart, I can't wait to watch you perform them."

"I'm glad you know all the lines, because I don't. I'm freaking out. I can't remember any of them," said Alex. He looked terrified. "You have to help me rehearse today."

Mason waved him away. "Man, you've got this. You rock. You're a star. You're a rock star."

"No, I don't. No, I'm not." Alex shook his head wildly.

Mason knew Alex well enough to know when his friend was doing his usual panicked routine. He had done the same thing before plays in the past. He was always a little anxious before every show. But in the end, he always pulled it off and did a great job. It was as if freaking out before the show was part of his acting method or something.

Mason laughed. "You know all the lines," he said. "The last few times we practiced, I didn't even have to feed any to you. You're going to be fine."

Alex didn't reply. He just kept shaking his head.

"Besides," Mason continued, "I need you to help me train just one more time. I think I have a real shot at —"

"Didn't you hear me?" interrupted Alex. "I don't remember any of the lines. The play is Saturday night."

"You're just panicking like you always do," said Mason.

Alex ignored what Mason had said. "Didn't I just hear you say you're going to race in the two hundred?" he asked. "Isn't that what you've been training for?"

"Yeah . . ." replied Mason.

"Well, you got it. You got in the race. Mission accomplished," said Alex. "Now it's my turn."

"But I have a chance to place," said Mason. "Maybe even win. I just need to train a little more."

Alex rolled his eyes. "Unbelievable," he said.

"What about tomorrow? Friday?" asked Mason. "The race is Saturday, and I shouldn't train the day beforehand anyway. We can run lines then."

"Friday is dress rehearsal," said Alex. "That's too late. It's today or nothing."

"Same here," said Mason.

"Dude, now you're just being greedy," said Alex. He frowned and shook his head. "You got in the race. Why do you have to win? Dumb jocks. Always so competitive."

"Hey," said Mason. It was the first time his best friend had ever called him that name and meant it. Mason wasn't going to let him get away with that. "Well, at least I'm not a drama geek," he said. "Always . . . full of drama."

Alex narrowed his eyes. "Whatever," he mumbled. With that, he turned and stormed off.

CHAPTER 9

BAD IDEA

Mason was still fuming as he rode his bike down the bumpy dirt trail.

Alex is supposed to be my best friend, Mason thought. *How could he let me down like that? He knows how important swimming is to me. Why else would I have worked so hard all this time?*

Mason realized that they hadn't worked as hard on Alex's lines. But that was different. Alex knew the play backward and forward. He was panicking for no reason. Mason had a real chance to win the two-hundred-meter race.

All I asked for was one more day of training. What's the big deal? Mason wondered as he rode down to the lake. *So my best friend let me down when I needed him most. Whatever. I don't need him to practice.*

Mason pulled to a stop where the trail curved toward the shore. He walked his bike to the edge and leaned it against a tree. He pulled off his backpack and dug out his swim cap and goggles. Once he was suited up, he waded out into the shallow water.

The water lapped against his shins. The wind had picked up again, and the lake was churning. Luckily, as Alex and Mason had discovered before, it wasn't as rough in the inlet beside the island.

Mason knew this wasn't the brightest idea. After all, he was breaking the first and only rule of the buddy system — swimming without a buddy.

But I'm an excellent swimmer, Mason thought as he adjusted his goggles to fit tighter. *Besides,*

Alex and I have trained almost all week in this very spot.

Mason knew that from this shore to the island was a distance of about two hundred meters. That meant he could swim one practice race to the island and one on the way back for a total of four hundred meters. *I've got this . . . with or without Alex and the Green Avenger,* he told himself.

With that thought, Mason dove in and began to swim. This time he planned to work on his speed and form at once. During his time trial, he'd had trouble doing both at the same time. His form had been good until he'd poured on the speed. A few slipups had cost him precious seconds. If he could work on swimming as fast as he could and maintain perfect form, Mason knew he could win.

Arm over arm, Mason slowly built up speed. He was a sprinter, so he knew he could maintain speed and good technique for a few laps at least. It was end of the time trial that had given him trouble. When he began to get tired, he would have to concentrate on his form even more. That would be the final part of his training.

Mason didn't know if it was the rough water or his breakneck speed. Whatever it was, he felt himself tiring earlier than usual. Almost immediately, his technique began slipping.

This was it. Mason imagined splitting his brain in two. Half would concentrate on speed while the other half worked on performing each stroke, each breath, each kick perfectly. It was difficult at first. He made a few stuttered strokes, and his feet bumped together once.

Then, after a few more strokes, he was doing it. Mason kept perfect speed and form. He felt like a great white shark, cruising just under the ocean's surface. He was in the zone. He was a machine.

Mason glanced up to see where he was. To his surprise, he was barely halfway to the island. He felt as if he'd swum farther than that. He didn't let the distance bother him, though. *It just means more training time,* he thought.

Stroke, stroke, breathe. Stroke, stroke, breathe.

Mason pushed himself harder and harder. He didn't know where it came from, but he was able to kick up the speed. His heart pounded and his muscles burned, but he kept his focus. Each stroke, kick, and breath was perfectly timed. He had to be nearing the island.

Mason glanced up again. The island shore was closer now, but it was still farther than he'd expected.

A gust of wind suddenly whipped over him, and a large wave crashed over his head. He missed a stroke and immediately ducked his face back into the water. He tried to concentrate on the strokes again, but it was becoming more difficult. He felt a tiny spark of panic in his gut, and it distracted him. The wind had picked up, and he was making slow progress.

Mason tried to push back his thoughts. He was closer to the island than he was to the shoreline, but he was tiring fast. He gave up trying to simulate a two-hundred-meter race. He didn't need to make good time, he just had to get there while he still had the energy.

Stroke. Stroke. Breathe.

Mason felt himself slowing. He kicked harder but found it more difficult to stay in position. The lake water seemed alive as it rocked him back and forth. Most of his energy was spent fighting whitecaps rather than moving forward. He no longer even attempted to concentrate on form or speed. His goal now was just to get to the island safely.

After several minutes, Mason decided to tread water. He needed to catch his breath. He dropped his feet and was surprised when he felt them sink into the muddy lake bottom. He had made it to the shallow water surrounding the island.

He stood and waded through waist-deep water the rest of the way to the shore. As he climbed out of the water, he wheezed and stumbled forward. He slumped onto a thick log. It was the same log that he and Alex had sat on just days before.

I really wish Alex was here right now, Mason thought.

He looked out over the rough surface of the lake. The shore of the mainland seemed like it was a mile away. Mason's heart pounded as he continued to pant. Just the thought of trying to cross the lake again filled him with dread.

"Okay," Mason said to himself. "This was clearly a bad idea."

CHAPTER 10

DRAINED

The treetops swayed overhead as Mason continued resting on the log. He was hoping the wind would die down while he caught his breath. Once that happened, he felt confident that he could swim back to shore safely.

Mason waited almost an hour, but the weather didn't improve. Even worse, black clouds began to roll in overhead. They covered the setting sun, causing the sky to darken faster than normal. *If I wait much longer,* thought Mason, *I might have to deal with rain as well as strong winds.*

He thought about spending the night on the island. He and Alex had camped there many times, after all. Of course, back then they'd had a tent and their parents' permission.

Mason's parents knew he was out training on the lake like usual this evening. But they didn't know that Alex wasn't there with him. He had been so eager to get in more training that he hadn't thought to mention it. Then again, part of him knew that his parents wouldn't have let him go if he had mentioned it. And he knew they would start to worry if he didn't make it home soon.

Mason stood and stretched his arms. He waded out into the lake. When the water was up to his waist, he dove in. The water was just as choppy as before, but Mason was confident he could make it through the rough waves. After all, he had made it through the first time.

This time, however, he wasn't going to sprint. He decided to take it slow and steady across the whitecaps. He didn't want to risk tiring himself out before he reached his destination.

Things went well for a while. Although the surface was just as turbulent, he cut through it steadily. He knew it would take longer this time, but he concentrated on his technique anyway. Even if he wasn't sprinting, he didn't want to make any wasted strokes.

Mason glanced up between strokes and saw that he was about a third of the way across. Even though he was pacing himself, he felt fatigue starting to creep into his limbs.

Maybe I should've rested longer on the island, he thought.

But as far as Mason was concerned, he had come too far to turn back. He slowed his pace, trying to conserve energy.

The lake surface was starting to become more turbulent. From the island, the waves didn't look very choppy. But now that Mason was in the thick of it, he had to struggle to stay in position. The waves crashed into his face, and he had to kick harder to keep his body level.

Mason didn't feel like he was making much progress. In fact, he felt as if he was swimming in place. He popped his head up and glanced at the shore. He found renewed hope when he saw that he was halfway there.

But then it began to rain.

Between the splashes from his kicks and the turbulent water, Mason hardly noticed the rain at first. But then he felt heavier thumps on his head and shoulders. When he glanced up again, he found that it was raining so hard it was difficult to see the shore. The rain was like a curtain blocking his vision.

Mason felt panic well up inside him. *I should have never come out on the lake alone,* he thought. *Swimming without a buddy . . . how dumb was that?*

Now he was out in middle of the water, tired, sore, and worst of all, alone.

Mason stopped swimming. He turned onto his back and began to float. He had to rest and calm down. Every swimmer knew that the worst thing to do in an emergency situation was panic. But it was difficult to settle down in the churning water. The rain made it hard to breathe without getting a mouthful of water. Still, Mason cracked his lips and took long breaths. After a moment, he felt himself relax.

I can do this, Mason told himself. *I'm a great swimmer. A competitive swimmer. Whether it's in a pool, in a lake, or falling from the sky, water is water. Water is my friend.*

Mason had just managed to calm his mind when a large wave washed over him.

CHAPTER 11

STORMY WATERS

Mason coughed out a mouthful of water and flipped from his back to his stomach into swimming position. He reached forward to make a stroke, and his hand struck something hard. Mason grabbed the object. It felt like a long tube. He looked up and saw what it was — a paddle.

"I knew you'd be stubborn enough to try this alone," Alex shouted. He frowned as he bobbed up and down, sitting inside the Green Avenger.

Mason clung to the paddle and caught his breath. "Thanks," he gasped.

"Grab onto the side," instructed Alex. "I'll paddle us to shore."

Without a word, Mason did as he was told. He held tight and was pulled along as Alex paddled the craft. The kayak bobbed in the rough water.

In almost no time at all, Mason felt the mud under his feet once more. They had reached the shore. He didn't know if he had been closer than he thought or if the kayak traveled faster than he swam. Either way, he was glad to finally be out of the lake.

Alex hopped out of the boat and pulled it to shore, and Mason waded out after him. "Let's leave the kayak behind these bushes," said Alex. "I'll come get it when it stops raining."

Mason helped Alex slide the kayak beside a stand of junipers. Then he removed his cap and goggles. He shoved them into his backpack and picked up his bike. Alex hiked up the trail while Mason pushed his bike along behind him.

"Thanks again," said Mason. "I didn't think I was ever going to make it back."

"Imagine how rough it is out toward the old dam," said Alex. "Good thing you didn't swim there alone."

"I may be a dumb jock," said Mason, "but I'm not that dumb."

Alex's shoulders fell. "Man, I'm sorry about that," he said. "I shouldn't have said that. And I shouldn't have left you hanging like that."

"Hey, it's my own fault," said Mason. "I'm the one who broke the number-one rule of the buddy system."

Alex rubbed the back of his neck. "Yeah, but I knew this race was important to you. We should've trained together one more time. It wouldn't have taken that long."

Mason pointed at the sky. "We would've been rained on, and you would've been soaked again," he said.

Alex pinched the front of his sopping T-shirt and pulled it away from his chest. "Good thing that didn't happen," he said, smirking.

Mason laughed. "I'm the one who should be sorry, though," he said. "I should've been more supportive. I mean . . . I know that you know all the lines, and you were just freaking out about being the lead all of sudden. But still, I should've realized that was scary for you."

"I wasn't freaking out," Alex said.

Mason smiled. "Dude, you were *so* freaking out," he said.

"Okay, maybe a little," admitted Alex. "But I'm better now."

"If you let me borrow some dry clothes, I'll help you run lines," said Mason.

"Are you sure?" asked Alex.

"Yeah," agreed Mason. "Let's get you ready for your big night."

"But are you ready for your race?" asked Alex.

Mason rolled his sore shoulders. "Maybe after a full day of not even seeing water," he said, smiling.

"Dude, you're still going to shower, right?" asked Alex. "If not, let me know so I can move my desk away from yours in history class."

Mason laughed. "Deal."

CHAPTER 12

WITH THE BIG FISH

That Saturday, Mason stretched his arms as he padded over to the starting blocks for the two-hundred-meter freestyle race. He found his lane, stepped onto his platform, and shook out his arms once more. Mason bent into a starting position.

"Good luck, dude," Mason said to Josh, who was standing to Mason's right on his own starting block.

"So now we'll finally see if you can swim with the big fish," Josh said, smiling at Mason. "Good luck."

Even though he had rested the entire day before, Mason was still a little sore. He felt better knowing that he would swim his toughest race when he was fresh. He hoped that small advantage would help him with his time.

"On your marks!" shouted the race official. "Get set . . ."

BEEEEEEEEP!

Mason sprang off his starting block. He spread his arms in front of him and felt the cool water surround him. He could tell that he'd barely made a splash.

A perfect start, he thought.

He swam underwater for a few feet and then surfaced. His body was already going through the motions.

Stroke, stroke, breathe.

Mason relaxed his mind as his body kept perfect form. He never had to concentrate too much on technique at the beginning of a race. That would come later. Now, he just needed to focus on pacing himself. Although he was anxious to win, he didn't want to burn out too early.

As he approached the opposite edge, Mason dove underwater. He somersaulted, and his feet found the wall of the pool. He pushed off hard and felt his body rocket through the water as he spun back into position. It was a perfect flip turn.

Mason kept a steady pace and maintained perfect form. He performed the next three flip turns with equal perfection. Now it was time to increase the speed.

Stroke, stroke, breathe. Stroke, stroke, breathe.

Mason zipped down his lane and reached the pool's edge. He executed another great turn. Now he was more than halfway done. Time to dial it up some more.

Normally at this point, Mason would have to concentrate hard to keep everything running smoothly. Adding speed would take away from part of his mind that was executing the proper technique. In this race, Mason certainly had to concentrate, but he wasn't struggling like he had in the past. All of his hard work and training were finally paying off. Mason had spent so much time swimming in the rough lake that now he felt as though he was gliding smoothly through the water.

After another turn, Mason added more speed. He didn't know if he was in the lead, but it sure felt like it. In fact, he felt as if he was the only swimmer in the pool. Any noise from the crowd was drowned out by the sound of the water rushing by his ears. He was only aware of his speed, his form, and the fact that he had just two laps to go.

Stroke, stroke, breathe. Stroke, stroke, breathe.

Mason turned into the final lap of the race. Now it was time to sprint to the finish. His heart pounded. He took deeper, faster breaths. He moved his arms smoothly, and he didn't miss a stroke. He kicked harder and faster and continued to stay level, willing every last bit of energy into his limbs.

Stroke, stroke, breathe, stroke, stroke, breathe.

Mason zipped through the water as he neared the finish. He felt as if he'd never swum faster.

Finally, he slapped the edge of the pool with his hand. He popped his head out of the water and glanced to either side. He was the only one there.

For a microsecond, Mason imagined that he'd really been swimming alone. *Or maybe I took so long to finish the race, everyone else has already gone home,* he thought.

Just then, the swimmer in the lane next to him hit the edge. It was Josh. The other swimmers quickly followed. It took Mason a second to realize he had won the race.

Coach Wilson and Mason's teammates rushed over to the edge of the pool.

Mason hauled himself out of the water and was greeted with high fives and fist bumps. They congratulated Josh as well. After all, their team had taken first and second place in the two-hundred-meter freestyle.

As the swimmers returned to the team's area, Josh extended a hand to Mason. "Good job," Josh said.

Mason shook Josh's hand. "Th-thanks," said Mason. This time Mason didn't try to hide the fact that he was out of breath.

"Hey, don't get too comfortable being the team's best distance swimmer," Josh said with a grin. "Looks like I have some training to do myself."

* * *

After the swim meet, Mason had just enough time to get home, shower, change his clothes, and eat. Then he and his parents got in the car and drove back to Gilmer Junior High School. They took their seats in the dark auditorium and waited for the school play to begin.

Mason applauded as the lights came on and the curtain opened. He even threw in a whistle as his best friend took the stage.

Alex wore a shining suit of armor. He clutched a knight's helmet with one hand and gripped a long sword with the other.

"The dragon sword!" shouted Alex. He raised a sword high above his head. "Forged in Atlantis. Bewitched by the dark wizard, Shantor. And honed to a fine edge by a red dragon's fiery breath!"

Mason silently mouthed the words as his friend recited them onstage. Then Mason held his breath as Alex paused. He seemed to take a little too long examining the sword's sparkling blade.

Alex turned to the audience and smiled. "The sword of my father!" he shouted.

Relieved, Mason exhaled and enjoyed the rest of the performance.

ABOUT THE AUTHOR

Michael Anthony Steele has been in the entertainment industry for twenty-two years. He has worked in many capacities of film and television production from props and special effects all the way up to writing and directing. For the past nineteen years, Mr. Steele has written exclusively for family entertainment. For television and video, he wrote for shows including *WISHBONE*; *Barney & Friends*; and *BOZ, The Green Bear Next Door*. He has authored more than one hundred books for various characters and brands including Batman, Green Lantern, Shrek, LEGO City, Spider-Man, Tony Hawk, The Hardy Boys, Garfield, Night at the Museum, and The Penguins of Madagascar. Mr. Steele can be contacted through his website: MichaelAnthonySteele.com.

GLOSSARY

capsized (KAP-sized)—turned over in water

confidence (KAHN-fi-duhns)—a strong belief in one's own abilities

dread (DRED)—fear of something you expect to happen in the future

endurance (en-DOOR-uhns)—the ability to do something difficult for a long time

natatorium (nah-tuh-TOR-ee-um)—an indoor swimming pool

rehearse (ri-HURS)—to practice in preparation for a public performance

rhythmically (RITH-mik-lee)—done in a repeated, steady pattern

simulate (SIM-yuh-layt)—to act out as a trial run

stamina (STAM-uh-nuh)—the energy and strength to keep doing something

technique (tek-NEEK)—a way of doing something that requires skill, as in arts or sports

DISCUSSION QUESTIONS

1. Mason and Alex have different interests, but they are still great friends. Do you think the boys would be better friends if they shared the same interests? Why or why not?

2. At the end of the book, Mason accomplishes his goal of competing in a two-hundred-meter race, but he had to work hard to get there. Talk about a time when you worked hard to accomplish something.

3. To show support for his friend, Mason goes to Alex's play. Discuss what it means to be supportive of a friend. How do you show support?

WRITING PROMPTS

1. We all make bad decisions once in a while —
   like Mason deciding to swim alone in the lake.
   Write about a time when you made a bad
   decision. How did you feel afterward?

2. Imagine you are Alex. Write a letter to Mason
   about how you felt when he said that he
   couldn't help you practice your lines before
   opening night.

3. One of Mason's teammates, Josh, teases him
   for not having great endurance at the beginning
   of the story. Write a paragraph explaining how
   you think Mason should have responded.

More About
SWIMMING

In **BUTTERFLY** and **BREASTSTROKE,** swimmers must use two hands to touch the end of the pool when they finish. In **FREESTYLE** and **BACKSTROKE**, swimmers only need one hand to touch the end.

Olympic swimming pools are **FIFTY METERS** long. Most swimming pools used for recreation are half that length — twenty-five meters.

Swimming has been an **OLYMPIC** event since 1896. Women have been allowed to compete since the 1912 Olympics. **SYNCHRONIZED SWIMMING** became an Olympic event in 1984.

While **FREESTYLE** is the fastest swimming stroke, **BREASTSTROKE** is the slowest.

It is easier to float in **SALT WATER** than in **FRESHWATER**, because things float better on denser surfaces. The more salt there is, the denser the water!

Whether you swim in the ocean, the pool, or your local lake, these fast facts will help you learn about one of the world's most beloved sports.

A **FALSE START** in swimming occurs when a swimmer dives into the pool before the gun or whistle sounds.

No one knows for sure how long people have been swimming, but **TEN-THOUSAND-YEAR-OLD** paintings of people swimming have been found in Egypt.

DIVING became an Olympic sport in 1904, while **SYNCHRONIZED DIVING** held its first Olympic competition in the 2000 games.

OPEN-WATER SWIMMING takes place outdoors in open bodies of water like oceans and lakes.

THE **FUN** DOESN'T STOP HERE !

FIND MORE AT:
CAPSTONEKIDS.com

Authors and Illustrators
Videos and Contests
Games and Puzzles
Heroes and Villains

Find cool websites
and more books like this one
at www.facthound.com

Just type in the Book ID:
9781434296375
and you're ready to go!